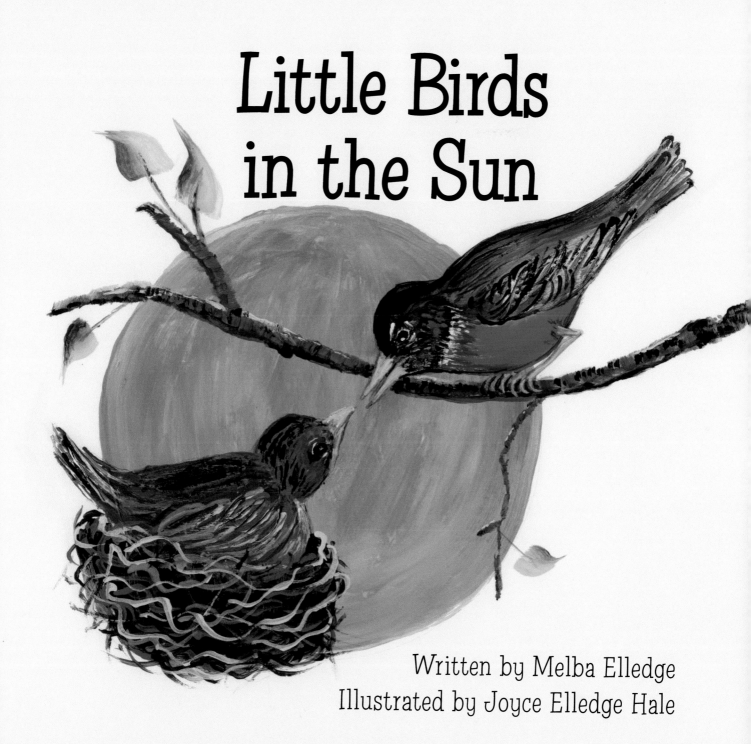

Little Birds in the Sun

Written by Melba Elledge

Illustrated by Joyce Elledge Hale

To order additional copies of this book, contact:
Xlibris
844-714-8691
www.Xlibris.com
Orders@Xlibris.com

ISBN: Softcover 978-1-4363-4704-4

Print information available on the last page

Rev. date: 12/27/2021

4

In our back yard, which was all green in spring's best finery of the season, a pair of robins worked. They were building their home. I could see them just outside my window. They chose the top of the tree, cut back from the summer before. There was a nice little spot in the fork of the tree where they could build a nest and raise their family. What the pair did not notice, however, was that there were no leaves or limbs above them to protect them when the sun became hot.

They brought twigs and grass, laid carefully, first the foundation of larger sticks, then a layer of softer grass, strings and whatever they could find.

They worked hard. First one would come, then the other, with their beaks full of building materials, gathered from our yard and the neighbor's nearby. The cool spring breeze seemed to make them hurry as they flew back and forth. Soon it was all completed.

Then it was time to lay the eggs, the prettiest blue eggs you ever saw, in the softness of their nest home, high above the ground, in the fork of the tree.

8

The time came to sit on the eggs to keep them nice and warm. Day and night the pair took their turn. In the day the sun shone brighter and brighter, as it climbed higher and higher into the clear blue sky. The spring's gentle breeze seemed to have slipped away. Now it was very hot . . . and the pair continued to sit on the eggs, keeping them just right so they would hatch.

Other birds flew by. They scarcely raised an eye, so intent were they on the job they had to do. The blue jay cocked its head and I thought he would surely frighten them away with his chatter and clatter.

Sometimes I walked out to get a closer look. No matter, they seemed to think, this is our home, our purpose in life. Day after day they took their turn. Each day they would turn the eggs in the nest.

One morning the sun seemed especially hot, the worms seemed especially tough, but as Mother Robin took her turn on the nest, there was a peep, chirp, and wow! there it was! their very first baby!

I watched as its head wobbled, its eyes blinked, and it looked neither like its mother or its father, but another mouth to feed.

The sun was ever so hot and the baby must be covered from the heat. The birds continued to take their turns. Father Robin took his turn, huffing and puffing as he returned on the wing. Before the day was over, there were three little darlings, all with open mouths ready to be fed.

On some days the sun did not shine. Instead the wind blew, rain came down, right on top of everyone—there was no place to go, no leaves to cover. Surely the little nest would be blown away, family and all. But the little pair stayed on. It was as if Father Robin would say, "Go dear, get yourself a snack, I'll sit awhile," and off Mother Robin would go.

It must have taken a can of worms each day—the little birds grew rapidly, quickly crowding their little nest. They sat on each other, chirped and cheeped, but mostly they slept and ate.

As the days went by, the sun climbed higher and grew hotter. Each day it seemed the mother got smaller and smaller, thinner and thinner, as she took her turn, both feeding and keeping her babies warm at night.

As the sun rose each morning the larger of the birdies would perch and totter on the edge of the nest, surely to plunge to its death. But Mother Robin would arrive with breakfast and gently push him safely back in the nest.

When the time came that they must learn to fly, it surely seemed too hot for flying lessons. However, the eldest took his turn, not that Mother Robin wanted him to. No, indeed. But what would a growing robin do all summer in such a small nest? So fly they must, and one by one, they did.

The first landed, very shaky, near the edge of the garden. Father Robin very quickly rewarded with a (juicy) morsel of earthworm. When he got his breath again he watched Mother Robin looking for another snack for the second of the brood. She found it just in time for the solo flight of the second, who plunged quite rapidly into the air, as it said, "Pe-e-e—e-p," and soon it landed in the grass.

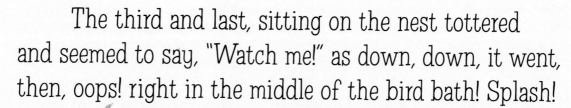

The third and last, sitting on the nest tottered
and seemed to say, "Watch me!" as down, down, it went,
then, oops! right in the middle of the bird bath! Splash!

"No, no, Baby, you can't swim!"
said Mother Robin as she coaxed
him out.

By this time the first began to hop, hop, hop.
"Look, look," he said, "I can jump!"

That night the little family stayed nearby
in the corner of the yard under a little tree, safely
hidden. As the big yellow cat went by, Father
Robin flew at it, scolding
him in no uncertain terms
to leave his family alone.
The blue jay
came by again.

17

The next day the birds practiced jumping and hopping. Then the next they really tried their wings. First, from the flower pots, up to the top of the fence. Then up to the clothes line. When they got on that they almost did flip flops, like monkeys on a bar. But soon their wings were strong enough to fly to the telephone lines.

All summer long they exercised. They looked so much like their parents by now that no one could tell them apart. Who was the baby or who was the parent? Everyone did their own breakfast, lunch and dinner.

Sometimes when it seemed the sun was the brightest and the hottest, I would hear the most heavenly song.

It was a duet, or a trio, or all at once, I would hear, "Cheerily cheer up! Cheerily cheer up!"

Wouldn't that brighten anyone's day? And there were other tunes I do not now remember.

But where was the sun? Now it seemed far away. When night came early, so did the shadows and the chilling winds. Leaves began to fall. It was harder and harder to find a juicy breakfast. Snow would soon be on its way. The Robin family must find a new home. They must follow the sun. God puts it in their hearts to do so. Yes, to the south they must go.

Hardly anyone noticed but as they suddenly were gone, we all knew we could look for them back in the spring. We knew that when they returned there would be more nests to build, more eggs to lay, more families to raise and more friends to enjoy.

Have you seen one of these in your yard? Perhaps next time they will build in your tree.

Printed in the United States
by Baker & Taylor Publisher Services